D0716102

First published in Great Britain in 2005
by Piccadilly Press Ltd,
5 Castle Road, London NW1 8PR
www.piccadillypress.co.uk

Text and illustration copyright © Fran Evans, 2005

All rights reserved. No part of this publication may be reproduced,
stored in a retrieval system, or transmitted, in any form or by any
means, electronic, mechanical, photocopying or otherwise, without
prior permission of the copyright owner.

The right of Fran Evans to be recognised as Author and
Illustrator of this work has been asserted by her in accordance
with the Copyright, Designs and Patents Act 1988.

Designed by Simon Davis
Colour Reproduction by Dot Gradations Ltd, UK
Printed and bound in Belgium by Proost

ISBN: 1 85340 806 9 (paperback)
EAN: 9 781853 408069

3 5 7 9 10 8 6 4 2

A catalogue record of this book is available from the British Library

Fairy Hill

Butterfly Fairy's Secret

❦ Fran Evans ❦

Piccadilly Press • London

It was a fresh autumn day on Fairy Hill.
The whole kingdom was aglow with warm colours.
This was an important time of the year
for the fairies. It was harvest time.

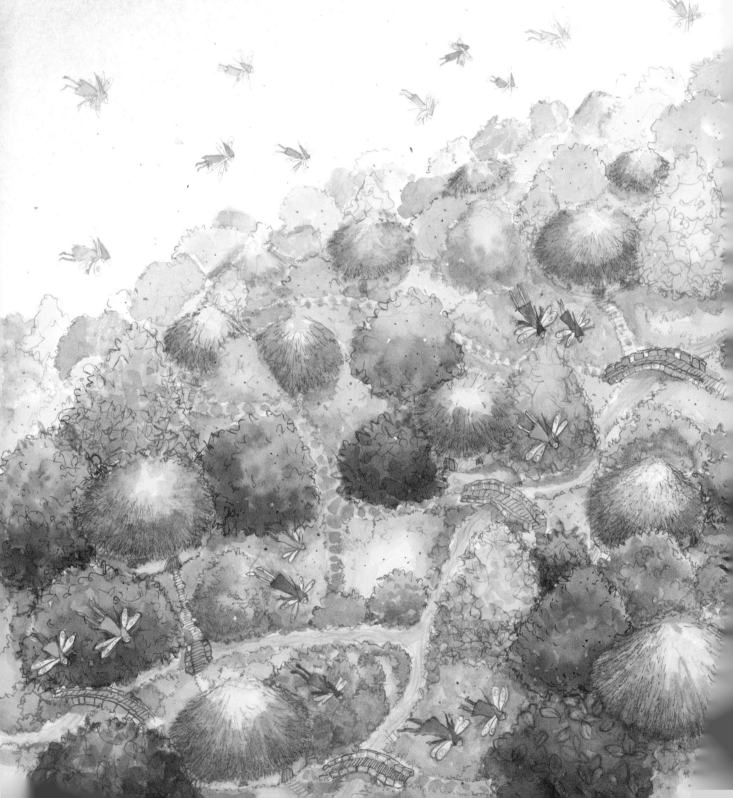

"That's better," sighed Butterfly Fairy.
But what was that noise?
Shuffle . . .
shuffle . . .
rustle, rustle . . .
A large woolly caterpillar was wriggling
around, half covered in a silky sack.

"Excuse me," Butterfly Fairy
asked shyly, "what are you doing?"
"Oh, hello," the caterpillar said, yawning.
"I'm trying to finish my cocoon. Please
don't be frightened," he added with a smile.
"I'm really not scary at all."

He had a friendly face.
"You look tired and hungry," Butterfly Fairy said.
"Here, have the last of my bilberries."
The caterpillar gobbled them up.

"Thank you, Butterfly Fairy, I feel
better already!"

Butterfly Fairy visited the caterpillar secretly every day, with bundles of goodies. She even took him the last of the nectar.

One cold, frosty morning she forgot to cover her tracks, and was followed. Her secret visits were discovered.

Later that day she was sent for by Queen Bee Fairy,
who spoke to her in a soft but stern voice.
"You know we need all the food we
can gather, Butterfly Fairy."
"Yes, but he's a friendly caterpillar who
needs food too," Butterfly Fairy pleaded.
"That may be," Queen Bee Fairy
replied, "but you must promise
me, no more secret visits."

"I promise,
Queen Bee
Fairy," she
whispered sadly.

Soon Fairy Hill was blanketed with snow. The fairies huddled around glowing fires, sipping warm honey, roasting nuts and telling stories.

One night, Butterfly Fairy was tucked up in her cosy bed, watching as snowflakes covered the tiny windows. "I do hope the caterpillar finished his cocoon before the snow," she thought, as she fell into a restless sleep.

A loud banging noise woke Butterfly Fairy.
Grasshopper Fairy leapt into the room.
"Our winter store is being *stolen*!" he shouted.

They raced through the tunnels
to join the rest of the fairies.

"I think it's that caterpillar," someone shouted.
"No!" Butterfly Fairy cried. "He'd never do such a horrible
thing! And besides, he must be asleep in his cocoon by now."

Grasshopper Fairy was the only one to nod in agreement.
Butterfly Fairy fled from the hall, followed by
Grasshopper Fairy.

"We must find the caterpillar before the others do," she said, packing her basket. "Come on, let's go!"
They flew over the winter woods, and at last found the caterpillar.

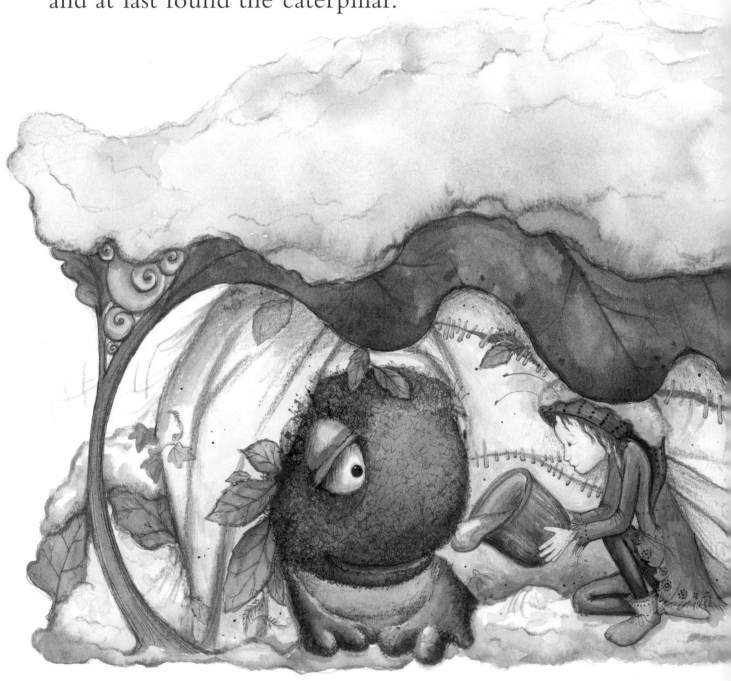

"Oh Caterpillar, are you all right?"
Butterfly Fairy poured a drop of honey into his
mouth to wake him up.
"All the better for seeing you!" whispered the sleepy
caterpillar. "But I do feel quite strange."

He stretched from head to tail,
and his cocoon ripped open . . .

"Wow!" gasped the two fairies. Out of the cocoon crawled the most beautiful moth. "*Brrrrrrr*," the moth said, shivering. "It's still winter! What's going on?" The fairies looked very worried. "Oh Caterpillar – oops, I mean Moth. . ." said Butterfly Fairy. "Our food is being stolen. Can you help? The others think it is you!"

The moth shook his wings.
"One good deed deserves another,"
he announced, in between
big yawns. "All aboard!"

They swooped over Fairy Hill, scouring the kingdom for the thief. On their second lap, Butterfly Fairy tapped on the moth's shoulder.

"Look! There's our food!" She pointed at a small burrow in the snow.

Suddenly, a greedy, brown mouse scampered
out, overloaded with berries.
"We've got to stop him!" exclaimed
Butterfly Fairy.

"Hold on!" yelled the moth, as he gathered strength and flew as quickly as he could towards the mouse.

The winter sun cast a shadow . . .

The mouse stopped in his tracks. Thinking the shadow belonged to a hungry owl, he dropped the berries and ran as far away from Fairy Hill as his stubby legs could carry him.

"Hooray! Hooray!
Moth has saved the day!" the fairies cheered.
Queen Bee Fairy stepped forward.
"Your kindness to the moth has helped us all, Butterfly Fairy."
And turning to the moth, she said,
"What a fine moth you are. How can we repay you?"

He yawned. "I wouldn't
mind a snooze."

That evening, Butterfly Fairy made the moth a bedtime
drink of warm honey and blueberry juice.
"Spring will soon be here," she whispered.

The moth snuggled into his bed of clover
and drifted off to sleep, dreaming of sunbeams.